HANSEL AND GRETEL

THE BROTHERS GRIMM

On the edge of a dark forest lived a woodcutter and his two children, Hansel and Gretel. After his first wife died the woodcutter married again. But his second wife was greedy and unkind and she did not love the children.

Though the woodcutter worked hard, he did not make enough money to feed his family. One night he said to his wife, "There is hardly enough food to feed the children tomorrow. What can we do?"

"They must find their own food," she answered cruelly. "Tomorrow we shall leave them in the forest."

The woodcutter pleaded and argued, but his wife would not listen. The children could hear the quarrel and Gretel began to cry. "Don't worry," Hansel whispered, "I have a plan."

Later that night Hansel crept downstairs and went into the garden. He quickly filled his pockets with white pebbles and quietly went back to bed.

In the morning their stepmother said, "Today we are all going to the forest." When they reached the dark forest, Hansel dawdled behind. Each time his stepmother's back was turned he took a pebble from his pocket and dropped it on the ground.

After they had walked for a long time the grownups stopped. "Hansel and Gretel, you must be tired now. Sit down and eat some bread and we will come and fetch you soon."

The children ate the bread and played for a while. Then they fell asleep under the trees. When they woke up it was dark and they were still alone.

"They've left us behind," sobbed Gretel. "We'll never find our way home. We'll be eaten by bears." But Hansel pointed to the trail of pebbles shining in the moonlight. He took Gretel's hand and together they followed the trail all the way to their home.

When they reached the cottage, their father hugged them tightly. He was happy that they were safe, but their stepmother was angry and sent them straight to bed.

"It's no good looking so pleased," she scolded the woodcutter loudly. "Tomorrow we must try again to lose them in the forest."

Hansel waited till everyone was sleeping, and then crept downstairs to collect more pebbles. But the door was locked. That night he lay awake, trying to think of a plan to save them from their stepmother's cruel plan.

"Let's spend the day in the forest again," their stepmother called the next morning, "Hansel, you carry the bread for lunch."

Just as before, Hansel dawdled behind the others. This time he dropped little bits of bread to mark the trail.

When they reached the middle of the forest their stepmother said, "Sit here and eat your bread while we chop wood."

Hansel and Gretel were tired from their long walk and soon fell asleep. When they woke it was dark and once again they were alone. Together they searched for the trail Hansel had made. But they couldn't find a single bread crumb. The birds had eaten them all!

In the heart of the dark forest, Hansel and Gretel clung to each other.

Soon the air grew cold and a hard frost formed on the forest floor. They huddled together at the foot of a tree. The birds took pity on them and dropped a quilt of leaves over the sleeping children to protect them from the cold.

In the morning Hansel and Gretel wandered through the forest until they came to a grassy clearing among the trees. Then they stopped and stared in amazement. Before them was a house made entirely of candy! It had gingerbread walls, windows made of sugar and a chocolate roof. It looked and smelled like Christmas and Easter all rolled into one. Hansel and Gretel were so hungry that they ran to the house and began breaking off bits to eat.

A very old woman called to them from the window. "Don't eat my house, children," she croaked. "Come inside and I will feed you."

Hansel and Gretel told the old woman how they got lost, while she fed them with delicious pancakes.

"Thank you," said Hansel when he'd finished eating. "Can I wash the plates for you?"

"No, no, child," said the old woman. "But you can sweep out that cage for me."

It was a very large cage, big enough for Hansel to crawl inside with a brush. Suddenly, the door clanged shut behind him and the old woman shrieked with delight. "Got you! A witch, a witch, that's what I am!"

The witch made poor Gretel her servant. Morning till night, she had to scrub and sweep and clean. But her plans for Hansel were even worse. "Ha! I'll fatten you up, my boy. Then one day soon I'll roast you for dinner."

Every day the old woman would go to the cage and peer in at Hansel. "Poke your finger through the bars," she would say. Then she would feel his finger to see if he was getting fat.

Hansel and Gretel noticed that the old witch could not see very well. So the next day, when the witch came to feel his finger, Hansel held out a chicken bone.

"Too thin, too thin," she snapped. "You'll never be fat enough to roast. I'll have to turn you into soup instead!"

The witch told Gretel to heat a big pot of water. "I want it very, very hot," she said, "so put lots of logs on the fire."

"The stove is ready," said Gretel after a while. "But I don't know if it's hot enough for you."

"Do I have to do everything myself?" snapped the witch. She hobbled over to the stove and bent down to look inside. Quick as a flash, Gretel gave her a mighty push. The witch tumbled into the stove and Gretel slammed the door behind her. There was a puff of purple smoke . . . but Gretel was too busy setting Hansel free to notice.

"Let's get out of this horrible forest," Gretel cried.

"Wait," said Hansel. "Father hasn't got enough to feed us. We must take something with us."

They made a sled out of the chocolate roof and piled it high with all the candy they could manage. They pulled the sled through the forest until at last they found the path leading home.

As the woodcutter's house came into view, they could see their father standing in the doorway. Their cruel stepmother had run away with a rich timber merchant and their father was very lonely without his children. When he saw Hansel and Gretel he was overjoyed and hugged and kissed them.

Hansel and Gretel and their father took the sled into town and sold all the candy. And they took home so much money that they never went hungry again.

The story of **Hansel and Gretel** is found in *Grimm's Fairy Tales*, edited by the German brothers Jakob and Wilhelm Grimm in 1812. Jakob and Wilhelm became interested in literary research as students at the University of Marburg. Perhaps under the influence of the Romantic movement in the arts, the brothers decided to collect the folk tales and songs of the German people and preserve them in written form. In later years, Jakob wrote the *German Grammar* (1819–1837) and both brothers worked on a German dictionary.